MEET MISS FANCY

IRENE LATHAM

illustrated by JOHN HOLYFIELD

putnam

G. P. PUTNAM'S SONS

For my dear friend Pat, who never
doubted I would find a way to tell this story.
And for Liz & Jim Reed, my beloved
"Birmingham" parents.—I.L.

To my "sister" Debbie, thank you for
giving me enough love and support
to last ten lifetimes. —J.H.

G. P. PUTNAM'S SONS
an imprint of Penguin Random House LLC
375 Hudson Street
New York, NY 10014

G. P. Putnam's Sons is a registered trademark of
Penguin Random House LLC.

Library of Congress Cataloging-in-Publication Data
is available upon request.
Manufactured in China by RR Donnelley Asia Printing Solutions Ltd.
ISBN 9780399546686
10 9 8 7 6 5 4 3 2 1

Design by Eileen Savage. Text set in DTL Documenta.

FRANK LOVED ELEPHANTS. He loved drawing elephants and talking about elephants. He loved their hosepipe trunks and their flap-flap ears, their tree-stump feet and their swish-swish tails. But not once, not ever, had Frank seen a real elephant.

Which is why Frank leaped out of his seat when his mother told him about Miss Fancy. "Just think, Frank—an elephant!"

"That's right," Reverend Brooks said. "She's retiring from the circus and moving to Avondale Park."

"An elephant?" Frank could barely breathe. *"Here?"* Avondale Park was just two blocks from their house.

"If the city can raise enough money. There's going to be a penny drive in all the schools. Starting immediately."

Frank got right to work collecting pennies. He prayed that the money from his school and all the other schools would be enough to bring Miss Fancy to Birmingham.

It was!

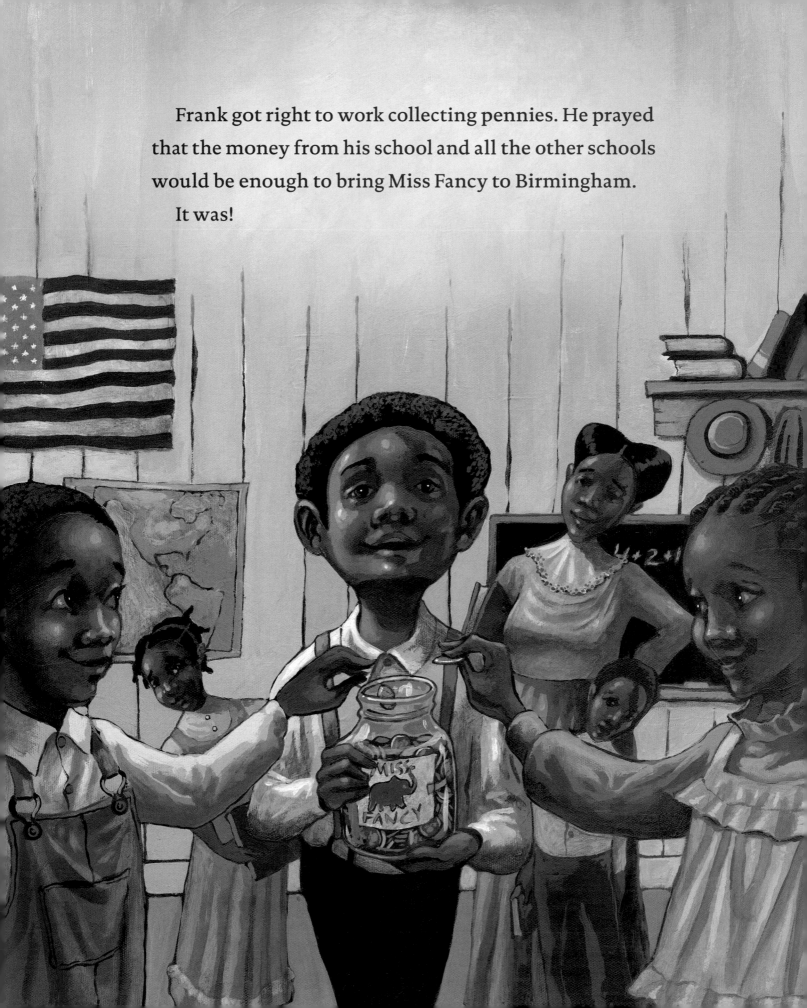

On the day Miss Fancy arrived at the train station,
Frank cheered with the crowd as the engine hissed to a stop.
When Miss Fancy stepped onto the platform, he gasped.
She was wider than a house, and her wrinkly skin was the
exact same shade as a thundercloud. When she trumpeted,
it made the train whistle sound like a toy.

Frank followed as the mayor, some police officers, and the elephant keeper, Mr. Todd, paraded Miss Fancy to her new home. When they reached Avondale Park, Frank stopped in front of a small sign.

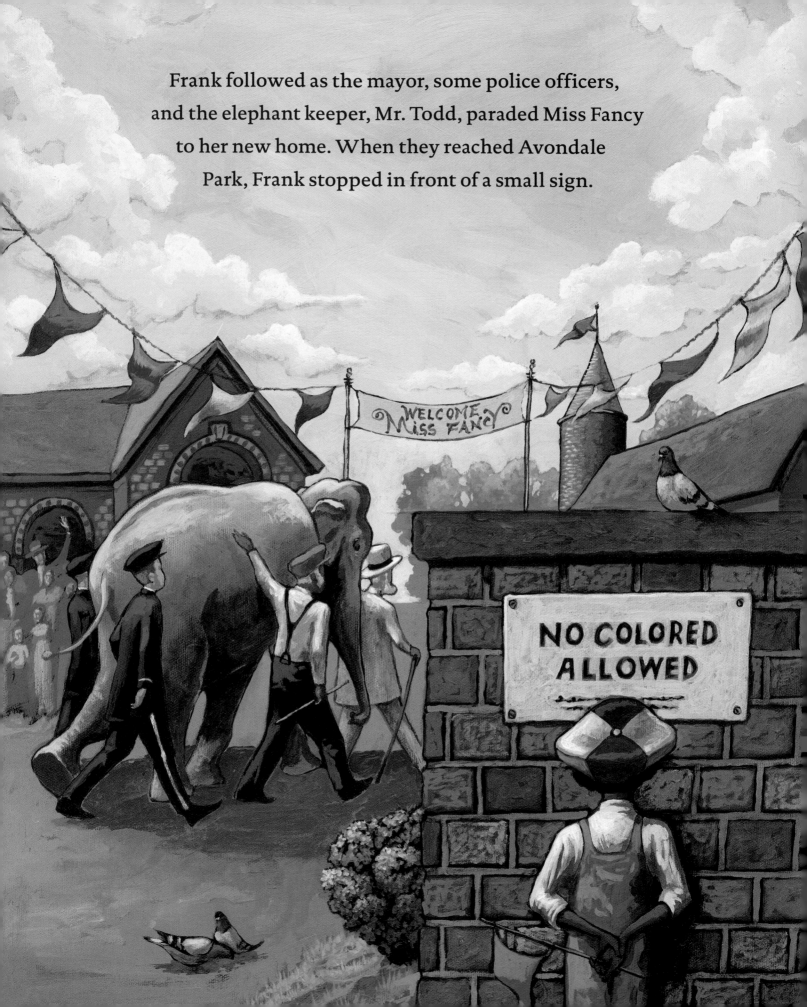

"Mama, how am I supposed to feed Miss Fancy a peanut if I can't get close?"

"Listen, Frank. I know it's not right, but it's the law. Change will take time."

Frank waited for the crowd to thin. Finally, when the park was nearly empty, he climbed a tree and whistled at Miss Fancy. When she turned her head, Frank drew his arm back and sent the peanut flying into Miss Fancy's yard. He grinned as she wiggled her trunk like a fishing line and popped the peanut into her mouth.

Frank visited Miss Fancy every day. It was fun, but she was still so far away. He wanted to stroke her trunk the way the other children did. He thought her skin might feel like tree bark.

Each night, Frank's mother read to him the latest news. Miss Fancy tossed hay at visitors with her hose-pipe trunk. She kicked over a fire hydrant with her tree-stump feet. Sometimes she pulled open the park gate. Her ears flap-flapped and her tail swish-swished as she strolled down neighborhood streets and peeked inside windows.

The elephant's adventures gave Frank an idea. If something as big as Miss Fancy could slip out of the park, then maybe he could slip *in*.

The next day, his stomach somersaulted
as he stood in front of the NO COLORED
ALLOWED sign. He looked left, then right.
A woman glared at him. No, his feet wouldn't
budge. It was against the law.

He walked around to the back entrance. "Mr. Todd?
Would it be possible for me to pet Miss Fancy?"

Mr. Todd shook his head. "Wish I could, but
it's not up to me. I might lose my job. Then where
would Miss Fancy be?"

Frank's whole body sagged.

But Frank wasn't giving up. On Sunday, he cornered Reverend Brooks. "If I could just meet her. Up close. There's got to be a way!"

"Maybe," said Reverend Brooks. "We could write a letter. To the City Commission."

Frank's eyes brightened. "We could ask them to let our church inside the park. For a picnic! And everyone could sign the letter."

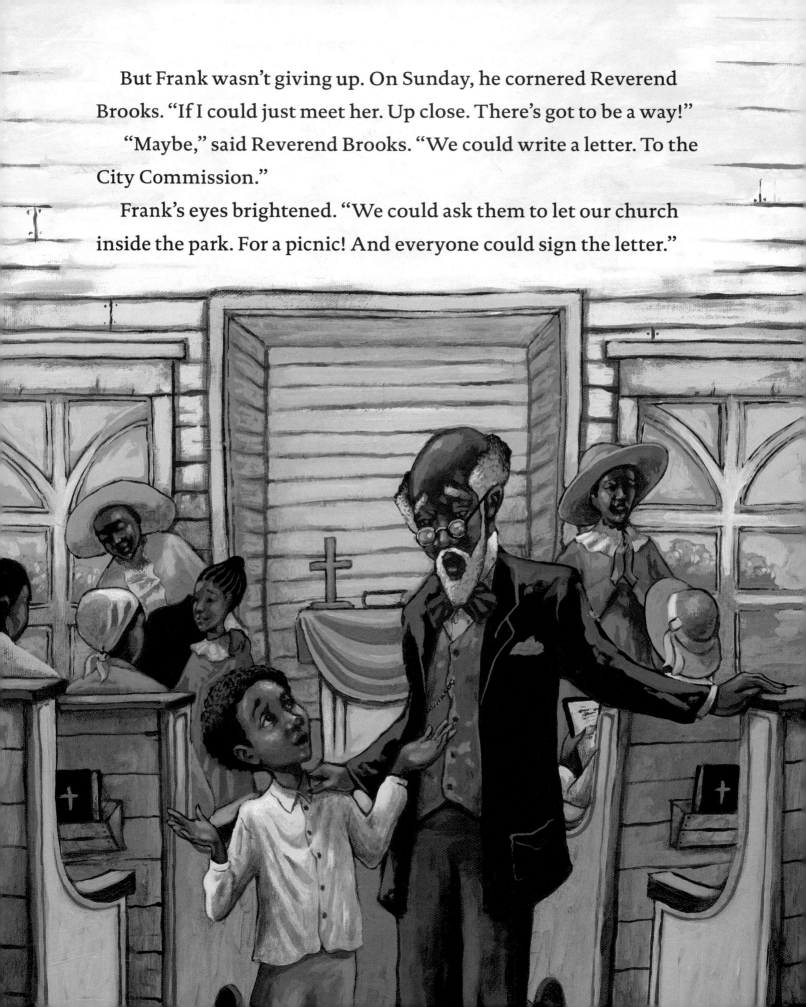

For the next week, Frank went door to door. Most people smiled and signed right away. Others scowled and said Frank was wasting his time.

Frank didn't rest until the letter was mailed. And then all that was left to do was wait.

Finally, it happened. Reverend Brooks pulled a letter from his pocket. "Good news!" he said. "'We are pleased to inform you that the city of Birmingham hereby approves your request to hold a picnic on the grounds at Avondale Park.'"

Frank whooped. Things were changing, just like his mother said they would. And now they were all going to meet Miss Fancy.

But the day before the picnic, Reverend Brooks appeared at Frank's door. "I'm sorry, Frank. There's not going to be a picnic. Some folks don't want us in the park. There could be trouble."

Frank swallowed. "Trouble" meant black people would be hurt or *worse*. He ran to his room and buried his head in a pillow. He'd tried everything he knew to get close to Miss Fancy. Everything.

And then it came to him.
There was only one thing left to do.
He ran all the way to the park.
"Next time you escape, Miss Fancy,
follow these peanuts!"

The next morning, Frank woke to a neighbor's
scream. "Someone call the police!"
Frank ran to the door. "Miss Fancy!"

He grabbed the bag of peanuts. By the time he got to the porch, Miss Fancy had wandered across the yard. Frank gulped as she trampled through his mother's patch of petunias. He followed as Miss Fancy nibbled Mrs. Harper's lawn. He giggled when she left behind a big smelly mess.

As she turned the corner, Frank's eyes widened. Didn't Miss Fancy see the cars coming? Didn't she know how dangerous that intersection was? He had to get Miss Fancy back to the park before she got hurt.

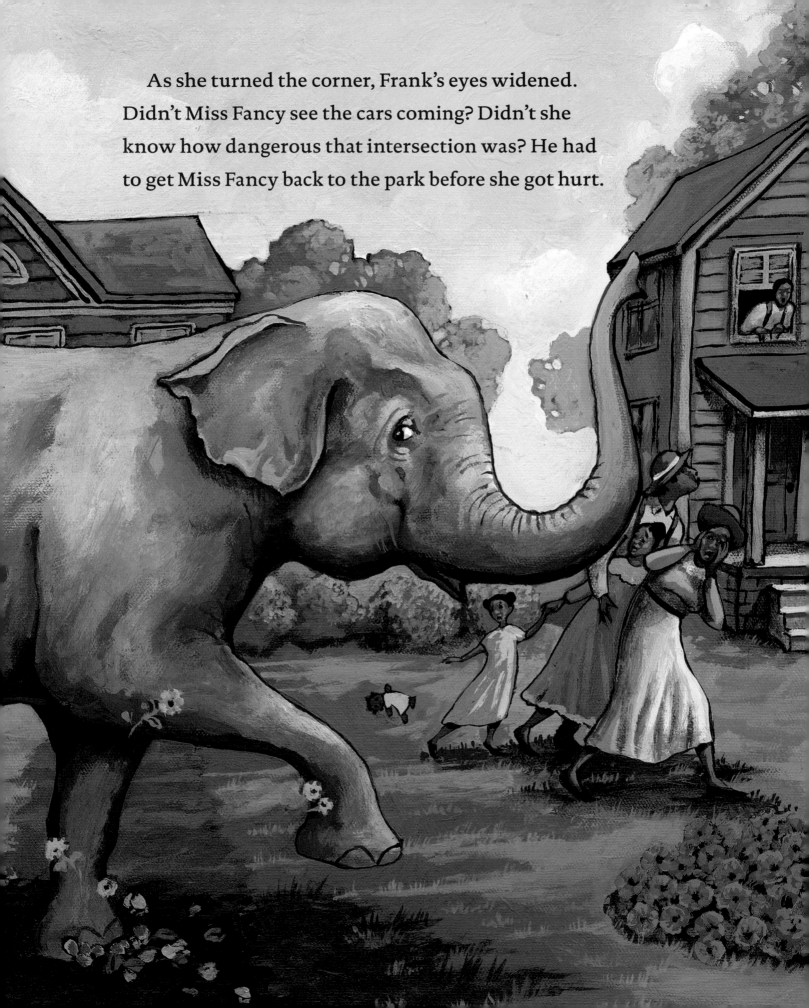

He raced in front of her, dropping one peanut, then another.

When they got back to the park, they were met by a police officer. "Good job, son."

Frank nodded but didn't speak. The NO COLORED ALLOWED sign glinted in the morning light. His time with Miss Fancy was almost up.

"Sir," he said. It was now or never. "Would it be possible for me to pet Miss Fancy?"

The officer studied Frank for a long moment. "How would you like a *ride*?"

A *ride*? Frank's breath caught. He'd seen white children riding Miss Fancy, but he never really believed he might get to ride, too.

As Mr. Todd helped Frank climb up Miss Fancy's tree-stump feet, her tail swish-swished. "You'd make a great elephant keeper," Mr. Todd said.

Frank grinned. The higher he went, the louder his heart thumped. When he straddled her neck, she lifted her hosepipe trunk and her ears flap-flapped. He stroked the skin on her head. It didn't feel like tree bark at all. More like Frank's favorite pair of shoes.

Frank laid his head against Miss Fancy and breathed in her mud-puddle smell. The sun warmed his shoulders as they paraded right past the gates of Avondale Park.

AUTHOR'S NOTE

WHILE FRANK, his mother and Reverend Brooks are fictional, Miss Fancy was a real Indian elephant who lived at Birmingham, Alabama's Avondale Park for twenty-one years, from 1913 to 1934. Schoolchildren collected five hundred dollars' worth of pennies to help purchase her from the Hagenbeck-Wallace Circus. Approximately forty years old at the time of her arrival, Miss Fancy was a gentle animal, the star attraction at the park and much beloved by the community.

Miss Fancy actually had two keepers during her time in Birmingham: Dayton Allen and John Todd. In order to keep the narrative simple, I only included Mr. Todd, who served as an assistant until Mr. Allen resigned shortly after Miss Fancy's arrival. At that point Mr. Todd took over, and except for a relatively brief absence to serve in World War I, Mr. Todd cared for the elephant the rest of her years in the city.

In spite of Mr. Todd's efforts, Miss Fancy still escaped on at least twelve separate occasions. Avondale Park didn't have the secure fencing that modern zoos have—it was more like a cow pasture. Miss Fancy really did walk the city streets, nibbling lawns and peering in windows. Occasionally she was more destructive, uprooting fire hydrants and trees, and once she even knocked over the park cookhouse.

Due to segregation laws, African Americans were not allowed to visit Avondale Park. In July of 1914, the 16th Street Baptist Church, under the leadership of Reverend John A. Whitted, petitioned the Birmingham City Commission to allow its congregation to visit the grounds for a Sunday picnic. When the motion was approved, it caused such a stir among residents that the Avondale Civic League protested the decision. As a result, the church withdrew its petition.

As the Great Depression set in, the city of Birmingham was no longer able to afford Miss Fancy's care, so she was sold in 1934 to the Cole Brothers–Clyde Beatty Circus. They renamed her "Frieda" and introduced her to three other elephants. By 1935, she had been renamed "Bama," in honor of her time in Alabama. She toured with the circus for just two years before she was sold in 1939 to a zoo in Buffalo, New York, where she remained until her death in 1954.

A note about peanuts: elephants in the wild do not generally eat peanuts, but those in captivity—especially circus elephants—have been known to eat them. According to reports, Miss Fancy ate not only peanuts, but also popcorn, fruit and sandwiches brought to her by park visitors.

Today, Miss Fancy's legend continues at Avondale Brewing Co. in Birmingham, Alabama, where her image graces trucks and labels and T-shirts. In addition, a life-size sculpture of her is being erected in Avondale Park.

Special thanks to James L. Baggett, writer and head of the Department of Archives and Manuscripts at the Birmingham Public Library, who helps keep Miss Fancy's story alive by generously and enthusiastically sharing his extensive knowledge with others. This one is for you, Jim!

IMAGE COURTESY OF ALABAMA DEPARTMENT OF ARCHIVES AND HISTORY